1

The Moon Lies Fair

A Play

by Lowery Christopher Collins

The Moon Lies Fair

A Play

by Lowery Christopher Collins

THE MOON LIES FAIR,
A PLAY

Written by Lowery Christopher Collins

Copyright © 2020 by Lowery Christopher Collins

Ponderlake Publishing: www.ponderlake.com

Playwright and/or Royalty Information: www.ChristopherCollinsOnline.com

ISBN 978-1-7349926-3-2

The Moon Lies Fair

By L. Christopher Collins

Cast

Reno Brooks, male, 29-35

Wade Bowman, male, 29-35

Belinda Whitaker, female, 29-35

Annie Gallagher, female, 25-32

Yago Svoboda, male, 25-32

Nina Greene, female, 56-60

Harold Greene, male, 56-60

Marie Greene, female, 85-90

Zoe Vitale, female, 25-30

Jaclyn Burgess, female 29-35

Henry MacAulley, male, 45-50

Voice of Caller #1, female, mid-twenties

The Moon Lies Fair

Scene 1

Max's Café

At the table is a young man, late 20's, goatee, dressed in modern style. Approaching him are two young women approximately the same age.

Belinda.   Up so early, stud?

Wade.   You act like it's 7 a.m., princess.

He continues to eat.

Belinda.   It's just that you lead such a nocturnal life.

The ladies sit with Wade.

Wade.   And I hold down a day job. Every day. Like clockwork.

Annie.   It's a wonder your clock even works as much as you demand of it. Going, going, going without stop, without *sleep!*

Wade.   What is this. "Gang Up on Wade Day"?

Belinda.   That's every day, Wonder Boy. It's our hobby.

Wade.   Oh, I see. I am a pastime, someone to attack and deride? For kicks?

Belinda.   Pretty much.

Wade.   O.K.

Annie.   Does that bother you?

Wade.   Not in the least.

Annie.   Good.

Belinda.   So, how late were you out last night?

Wade.   I don't remember.

Annie.   Right. How late?

Wade.   4. 4:30. I don't know.

Belinda.   And what time did you have to be at work this morning?

Wade.   8:30. (*He continues to eat.*)

Belinda.   Ah, beauty rest.

Wade.   Do I look like I need it?

Annie.   Vanity. Vanity.

Wade.   A person is allowed one fault.

Annie.   Oh, Wade. You are so full of yourself.

Wade grins.

Belinda.   Let me guess. number 55 for this year.

Wade.   Nope.

Belinda.   56?

Wade.   Don't worry about it.

Annie.   Higher?

Belinda.   Higher?

Annie.   Are you trying to break a record?

Belinda.   Or die an early death?

Wade.   Don't worry about it.

Belinda.	You are something, Wade. Absolutely something. If we weren't such good friends, I'd be talking about you horribly. You're an A-class tramp.
Wade.	Well, I'm glad we're friends, then.
Belinda.	You know I love you. Just remind me never to drink after you.
Annie.	So, did you have any good calls, last night?
Wade.	You didn't listen?
Annie.	I do have a life, Wade. I can't listen to you offer advice to late-night losers every single evening.
Wade.	Those "losers" are my fan base.
Annie.	Excuse me. I can't listen to you offer advice to your late-night "fan base" every single evening.
Belinda.	I actually listened about 11.
Wade.	*(Surprised.)* Really?
Annie.	*(Surprised.)* Really?
Belinda.	Really. That woman with the really, really raspy voice had some major issues.
Wade.	Yep. More than I could help with. I'm not there to solve anything. Just to talk. Play a few tunes. Listen to people's ideas.
Annie.	I still don't see how you do it—or why you do it. You have a good job. Why keep up the radio show at night?
Wade.	Three reasons. *(He continues eating.)*
Annie.	With the first being . . . *(leading)*
Wade.	I can't let Finny down. He gave me that gig before I had much of anything else. It's sort of a mainstay of his line-up. It would crush him.
Annie.	With the first being . . . *(as if his reason was void)*
Belinda.	We can give him that. That makes sense in Wade's World.

Annie.   Okay. And two?

Wade.   Extra money.

The ladies laugh.

Wade.   What?

Belinda.   As if you need it.

Annie.   Mr. Never Without Several Hundred.

Belinda.   You have the job with the unnatural paycheck, Daddy Warbucks.

Wade.   I never said I needed it. I said, and I quote, "the *extra* money."
                      Who couldn't use *extra* money?

Belinda.   He's right again. That *is* what he said.

Wade.   Are you just looking for me to say something wrong?

Belinda.   It's a hobby, remember?

Wade.   Oh, yeah.

Annie.   And three?

Wade.   Three?

Annie.   The third reason?

Wade.   Oh, well, duh . . . What do you think?

Annie.   I knew it.

Belinda.   Oh, Wader, that is so sad. The women? Don't you realize that the
                      women who listen to you . . .

Wade.   Like you did?

Belinda.   That's beside the point. *(Continuing).* The women who listen to
                      you are pretty much pathetic.

Wade.   Thanks.

Belinda.	You know what I mean. Lonely hearts, weirdos, sexually deprived females.
Wade.	Hence, my mission on this planet.
Annie.	Give up, Belinda. It's no use.
Wade.	Look, I'm happy. I don't do what you would. Or maybe I *do* do what you would if you were me, but that's beside the point. I work hard during the day. I make money. I talk at night. And I talk sweetly. I reach the female population, and at least some of them like it.
Annie.	And have ways of showing their interest.
Wade.	They know what they're in for when they step up. No complications. No regrets. Just quiet time with the Midnight Sailor, searching together for the North Star.
Annie.	I'm getting sick.
Belinda.	Batten down your hatches, Ahab. The waves can get bumpy.
Wade.	I carry a life preserver and motion-sickness tablets. I'll be okay.
Belinda.	It's amazing. If I didn't know you so well, and especially if I hadn't known you for so long, I'd be disgusted.
Annie.	I am anyway.
Belinda.	If I'd just met you, I'd steer clear as the plague, but, Wade, I know you. Why do I have to be such good friends with someone who epitomizes everything I hate? *(laughs—and reaches over and hugs him.)*
Annie.	Careful.

Wade breathes on Annie.

Annie.	Hey! *(Laughs. Hits him on the shoulder.)*
Belinda.	Is Reno joining us today?
Wade.	He's supposed to. He's not feeling too well at all.

Annie.	Didn't he go to the doctor? Or could he not afford to after all the *insurance* premiums drained his budget.
Wade.	You bash me. Now you bash my job.
Annie.	Just the profession. *(Continuing nonchalantly)* Didn't he go to the doctor?
Wade.	Well, he's been putting it off. He called my cell at, well, it had to be early, a little before 9, and said he was going to have to cave in and go, but he planned to meet us here. He's a bit late, isn't he?
Yago.	Late for what? I'm never late. What are we talking about? *(a young man wearing a VERY loud Hawaiian shirt slides into the chair next to Annie, snuggling an arm around her. She recoils in disgust and brushes his arm off as if he were a bug)*
Wade.	Hello, Yago.
Belinda.	Hello, Yago.
Yago.	*(hurt)* What, no salutations from you, my dearest Annie? I'm hurt. I'm insulted. I'm...
Annie.	disgusting. *(speaking to an imaginary waiter)* Waiter? Virgin margarita, please. With tequila. Thank you.
Yago.	That's no longer a virgin, then, Annie dear.
Annie.	Please don't set me up for such potential jokes. And . . . stay away from me.
Belinda.	Focus, Annie.
Annie.	Oh, yes. Reno. Did he or did he not go to the doctor? *(completely ignoring Yago, who is pouting)*
Yago.	*(singing)* "Is you is, or is you ain't my baby?"
Belinda.	Yago, can you please get us something to drink? One virgin margarita for Annie and a diet cola for me . . . and turkey on wheat sounds good, too. A girl's gotta eat.
Yago.	You'd think I'm your . . . your . . .

Belinda.	Yago, you are. You work here. You're a waiter—and at the moment, our waiter.
Yago.	Oh, yeah. (*Pauses.*) Man, you can't let me live in a fantasyland— to be able to think I may be a friend and not a common servant?
Annie.	The order.
Yago.	(*as if he Igor from horror-film fame*) As you wish, Master. (*He hobbles off.*)
Belinda.	Back to Reno.
Wade.	I don't know what's wrong. He won't even tell me the symptoms, just that he hurts. He treats it like it's some big secret.
Annie.	A secret? Among us? There are none.
Belinda.	You'd probably be surprised.
Annie.	Is there something I don't know?
Belinda.	No, I don't guess. We just don't know everything about each other. It wouldn't be right if we did. For instance, take Wade . . .
Annie.	No, thank you.
Wade.	Do you hate *all* men?
Annie.	No, my *dad*'s a good guy.
Belinda.	Anyway, take Wade . . .
Wade.	I'm just here, eating my lunch, waiting to hear from my sick best friend, about to go back to the financial jungle—then to the radio station. Just leave me be.
Annie.	Aw, he's sensitive. (*Yago walks up with a tray of drinks.*)
Yago.	You're darn right I am—especially right here on my neck.
Annie.	Stop! It's not all about you, Yago.
Belinda.	We were talking about Wade being sensitive.
Yago.	I'm sure he is. Statistics show . . .

Annie.	Yago, I'm going to kick you now. Please, I beg you. stop.
Yago.	(*as he delivers the* drinks) Never appreciated. Always underestimated. Never taken seriously.
Annie.	What do you expect? You're named after a bottle of wine. A bottle of wine.
Yago.	So? Is that so bad?
Wade.	There are worse things to be named after.
Annie.	What? A walk through a puddle, *Wade*?
Belinda.	Annie!?
Annie.	What?
Belinda.	That was good.
Annie.	Thanks.
Yago.	So, for real, how's Reno? (*Wade's cell phone rings. He answers.*)

Scene 2

A few days later

A darkened living room

Hidden by the darkness are a couch, chair, table, and several drawings and paintings on easels.

There is a knock at the door. There is knock again. Again.

Reno.	(*In the darkness*) Hold on. (*He gets off the couch and moves toward a side wall for a light switch*) Hold on. (*He turns the light on. Reno is young man somewhere around 30-to-35. He is wearing sleep pants. He also has a large bandage on his lower right part of his abdomen. There is another*

	knock at the door.) Hold on. Please. *(He walks toward the door.)* Who's there?
Wade.	*(From the other side of the door.)* Environmentally friendly vacuum cleaners for sell. Only a small fortune. *(now obviously talking to someone else)* Ouch. Stop it. Don't ever pinch me.
Reno.	Wade. The point of recovery is to get rest. *(resting his head against the closed door)*
Wade.	*(still from the other side)* Come, on, Reno. It's your *bestest* friend in the whole-wide world, here to cheer you up.
Reno.	*(Starting to open the door)* All right. And who's the pincher you have with you? *(He opens the door. Standing in the doorway are Wade and Belinda.)* Wow. Since when do you guys travel together? Is there something I should know?
Belinda.	*(walking in)* Please, Reno. Don't assume too much. You know what they say. If you must know, I met Wade over here to check on you. I promise. we're in two separate cars.
Reno.	Of course. *(walking back to the couch, obviously weak)*
Wade.	We just wanted to see how you were feeling, bud.
Belinda.	We?
Wade.	Well, *I* was at least. I don't know about Nurse Ratched.
Reno.	Wait. Am I even here? *(looks at his owns arms and chest)* Yes, I am. Your gentle concern overwhelms me.
Belinda.	Aw, how are you getting along, sweetie?
Reno.	I'll be fine. There was really no reason for . . .
Belinda.	Don't worry. None of us really got a chance to come to the hospital. Everything happened so fast, and so much is going on . . .
Wade.	*Us?*
Belinda.	Get over it. It's old now.
Reno.	Like I said, there is really no reason for . . .

Belinda. *(not paying attention to him, but rather to the art work around the room)* Reno, dear, some of these are new works, aren't they?

Reno. Well, . . .

Belinda. I realize it's been a little while since I've been here at your place, but you've really been working on these.

Wade. These are good, buddy.

Reno. I appreciate the seal of approval, but they . . .

Wade. No, these are very good. *(focusing on one)* I really like this one.

Belinda. I am so glad you're getting some rest.

Reno. *(with his head in his hands)* Me, too.

Belinda. And Mr. Sobbel has given you time to recuperate.

Reno. Yeah, sick leave. It's still right after surgery.

Belinda. Still, very generous, doll. If I had surgery, I don't know if Valerie would be so open to the idea. I'd have to volunteer to work nights for a year. *(to Wade)* Before you begin, don't.

Wade. You underestimate me, Belinda. I'm admiring Reno's talent. You're not just goofing around here, Buddy. You've got something.

Reno. Thanks, Wade. Thanks.

Belinda. When do you have to be back at the office?

Reno. I don't know yet. It depends on how I feel and how much rest I get.

Wade. You know, Picasso, if you need anything, anything, you call me. My cell is with me 24-7. I even keep it on vibrate during the radio show.

Reno. I appreciate that, Wade.

Wade. Does the incision hurt?

Reno. It's just really sore.

Wade. Well, I wish I could do something. Ice cream? A massage therapist?

Belinda.   A massage therapist??

Reno.   I'm fine, Wade. Just tired. Really tired.

Wade.   I get 'cha, pal. I hate to just stop by and go, but I need to be at the radio station soon.

Reno.   That's fine, Wade. Thanks for stopping by. Both of you.

Belinda.   I'm not with him, honey.

Reno.   Right.

Belinda.   Have fun on your boat, Wade.

Wade.   It's a ship, Belinda. The Ship. I'm the Midnight Sailor. It's the Ship.

Belinda.   Happy sailing. I'm staying here with Reno.

Reno.   You are?

Wade.   Good luck, my friend. *(pats Reno on the arm, starts to leave)* Good luck.

Belinda.   You're needing some sleep, Reno. I'll help you.

Wade.   Adios. *(leaves)*

Reno.   Help me? I can just . . .

Belinda.   You sleep. I'll stay right here, and if you need something . . .

Reno.   Belinda, that's so kind of you, but . . .

Belinda.   But nothing. It's what I want to do.

Reno.   I'll be okay. I can just . . .

Belinda.   Don't be ridiculous, Reno. I'm here. I have some free time this evening. My friend needs help. I'm helping. End of discussion.

Reno.   *(at a loss—it is obvious that his weakened state is keeping him from a further argument)* Okay. Whatever you want. You know where everything is.

Belinda.   Yes.

Reno.   And I'll be in here, lying down.

Belinda.   And I'll be in here in this chair, reading. You need anything, just holler.

Reno.   Okay. If it gets late, and you need to go, just be sure to lock the door behind you.

Belinda.   Sure thing. Sweet dreams, dumplin'.

Reno goes into his bedroom. Belinda settles in with a book she finds

Belinda.   *(to herself)* The taste you have in books, Reno. *(She grimaces.)*

Eventually, she dozes off. The light fade to black.

Scene 3

Very dim lights come up on the same living room. A few hours have passed. Belinda is still in the chair; she is asleep. Reno comes out, still wearing sleep pants, and he is carrying some sort of light blanket or throw. He stops and stares at Belinda. She doesn't stir.
He drapes the blanket across his shoulder as if he is carrying a coat or sweater. He slowly walks around the room very slowly, shuffling his bare feet across the floor. He stops at one of his paintings and stares at it.

Reno.   *(to himself)* Picasso. *(He laughs.)*

Belinda breathes heavily in her sleep and makes a slight moaning sound. Reno looks over to make sure she is still asleep. He touches the canvas.

Reno.   *(to the painting)* What are you trying to say to me? What are you doing? *(He walks to another one.)* I mean, why? I can't imagine . . . I . . . you . . . come on. Talk to me. We're not done. Picasso, huh?

Reno begins to walk around the room again. Very suddenly and very quietly, he tosses the blanket in a wad at downstage center. He goes to a desk or a table and, again quietly, rummages through things until he pulls out some charcoal and some rags. He picks up a small battery-operated lamp and sets it up (and turns it on) near the crumpled blanket. He puts the charcoal and rags near the lamp. Then, he walks over and picks up a newly begun canvas from an easel. He takes it, too, to the lamp, sits cross-legged on the floor, and pulls the blanket across his shoulders as if he is Superman.

Facing the audience, he begins to draw on the canvas.

Reno. *(to the canvas)* Tell me your secrets. Let's see what's trapped in here.
(He continues to draw—and then suddenly stops and stares.)

He turns the canvas 90° and stares at it. He breathes heavily. Belinda also breathes heavily. Startled, Reno looks at her, looks at the canvas, looks at her, turns 90° from the audience so that he can see her—and continues to draw.

Reno. *(growls)* No, don't do that. *(He rubs the canvas as if he has made a mistake. Belinda shifts her position.)* No. *(He puts the canvas down and rubs his hands on his face in frustration. In the process, he accidentally gets charcoal on his face.)*

He gets up and stares at the canvas on the floor. He then goes over to a table and pours himself a drink. He stares at it, holds it above his head and stares at it some more, then downs it. He pours another drink, turns on the radio—soft music is playing, and returns to sit by the crumpled blanket. He carries his glass and a bottle. He notices the charcoal still on his hands and attempts to rub it off with the rags he has there.

When the song is finished, Wade's voice comes over the radio. As soon as Reno hears his voice, he looks over to Belinda to make sure that she is still asleep. She is. Reno stares straight ahead and sips his drink.

Wade. *(over the radio)* Hello, fellow travelers. Thanks for sticking with me tonight. For those of you who've just tuned it, I'm the Midnight Sailor, here to guide you through the rest of the evening, to play you some soothing music, to take your calls. We're just here together, making the most of our time. The subject is anything, life itself. The mood is love. The tone is quiet. I'm here, for you.

Belinda. *(frowning in her sleep)* . . . liar . . .

Reno. *(drinking)* You got 'em eating out of your hand, Wade.

Wade. The night is young. I have music perfect for you to curl up with a soft blanket and a bottle of wine to, while you relax and calm down after a long day. *(Reno looks at his hard liquor and soft blanket.)* While you're there all alone, remember you have someone to share the evening with. The Midnight Sailor is ready to set sail with you. It's 9.39 p.m., and the lines are open.

Reno. 9.39? Only 9.39? *(He looks at Belinda, who has become restless.)*

Wade. Here's some more music. Ladies, I am here for you.

Belinda.   *(in her sleep)* . . . never . . . never . . .

Reno stifles his laughter and picks up the canvas. He attempts to draw again. While the music—soft jazz— is playing, there is a knock at the door.

Belinda awakes immediately.

Belinda.   What? Oh. *(She does not notice Reno. She stumbles to the door and whispers.)* Who's there?

Yago's voice. It is I.

Belinda.   What? *(She opens the door.)* Yago? What are you doing here? It's, it's *(looks at her watch)* well, late.

Yago.   No, it's not. It's just 9.30. What are you doing here? *(He starts to come in.)*

Belinda.   I'm sitting here for Reno while he gets some sleep.

Reno.   Reno can't sleep.

Belinda.   *(startled)* Reno, you scared me. I didn't know you were up. Are you okay?

Reno.   I'm fine, Belinda. Just having a little insomnia. I just feel strange.

Yago.   Well, I'll bet so. You just had a knife in you, slicing away at . . . well, you get the picture.

Reno.   Yeah, I was there.

Belinda.   *(turning on the main lights)* Aw, you're drawing.

Reno.   Well . . .

Belinda.   And drinking. Reno, are you supposed to have that? I mean, you're still not well and all.

Reno.   I'd like to see someone stop me. *(He pours some more.)*

Yago.   Wow, I've never seen you like this, Reno. Mouthy, direct. It's . . . different . . . but in a good way.

Belinda.   In a good way? It's nothing like you. I like the old Reno better.

Reno.   He's on vacation until I feel better.

Yago.   On vacation? Cool. *(He laughs.)* Reno, I've been meaning to stop by and check on you. How you feeling, man?

Reno.   *(He holds up the glass.)* Better with every sip. It's absolutely amazing how well liquor works.

Belinda.   Reno, this is so sad. This isn't you. Come on. Let's put the booze away for now.

Reno.   *(holds the bottle close to himself)* No. It stays right here. It's mine. Besides, I am not drunk. I have a disgustingly high tolerance for the stuff. It's not fair. It would take at least three gallons to phase me.

Belinda.   So, why are you putting it away, then?

Reno.   Let me pretend, Madam. It just makes me feel better. Let me pretend it makes a difference.

He sits on the floor close to his blanket. He grabs it and wraps himself up in it. Belinda sinks into the chair and remains very still.

Yago.   *(after a few moments of uncomfortable silence)* Tell me about the operation. Do you remember much?

Reno.   I don't want to talk about it, Yago. I appreciate your concern. I really do. I know I have some great friends. Belinda has graciously given up her evening to sit here with me. Wade stopped by earlier to check on me. You're here to see how I'm doing. I can't express how much I thank you for all of it, but I really, really don't want to talk about the operation or the hospital stay or any of it. I know that makes me sound horrible, and I'm sorry, but I can't right now. Okay?

Yago.   That's cool, man. I'm cool. A man has to deal with this own life in his own way. Nobody can tell you how to drive your own car, man.

Reno.   Yeah.

Belinda.   Can I get you something, Reno?

Reno.   I'm fine, Belinda. Thank you. And thank you for being here.

Belinda.   By choice, honey. Free will.

Reno takes a drink, looks at the glass, and starts to softly cry.

Yago.　　　　Reno? *(Draws closer to Reno)*

Belinda.　　　Sweetie, are you all right? *(Draws closer to Reno)*

Reno.　　　　I'm fine, really.　Just tired. *(He looks at the canvas on the floor.)* I have a lot on my mind.

Yago.　　　　Oh, I didn't notice! *(He beings to look around the room.)* You've been painting some more.　Oh, wow!　Reno, these are good.

Belinda.　　　See, you have yet another fan. *(She sees the canvas on the floor.)* Oh, were you working some tonight?　That's why your face is covered in charcoal.

Reno.　　　　What? *(He tries to rub it off. Belinda helps.)*

Belinda.　　　So, that's the newest masterpiece?

Reno.　　　　Yeah, it's gonna be called *Tigress*, but it's barely started.　Can't get going.

Belinda.　　　Let me see. *(She reaches for the canvas.)*

Reno.　　　　I don't know.

Belinda.　　　Aw, hush.　Give me the goods. *(She takes the canvas, looks at it, frowns, turns it, stares.)* This is stage one, right?

Reno.　　　　Aw, give me the thing back.

Belinda.　　　Wait a minute.　I'm trying to figure this out.　Strange subject.　Hmm. *Tigress*? (Reno nods.) Hmm.

Reno.　　　　Well . . .

Belinda.　　　Strange, Reno.　I want to see where you go with this one.　I just can't . . .

Reno.　　　　Here. *(He hands her the glass.　She takes a drink.)*

Belinda.　　　Hmm.　Still. *(She finishes the glass with one gulp.)* Hmm.　It's getting better.

Reno.　　　　Like I said.　The power of the bottle.

Yago.　　　　How long have you been working on these?

Reno.   What? Painting? Several years.

Yago.   No, silly. This last batch. These are different, so much more intent.

Reno.   A couple of months.

Belinda grabs the bottle from Reno, takes the glass and the canvas and goes to her chair to study the work.

Yago.   I'm very impressed. I've seen a lot of crap in my time, and a lot of crap people tried to pass off as good, but this is good, really good.

Reno.   I don't know how good it is. I'm just a painter. I have to do it.   It drives me crazy if I don't. Whether it's good or great or would work better as firewood is beyond the point.

Yago.   I don't see how you find time.

Reno.   Just do. Have to.

Yago.   I guess.

Reno.   The time finds me. If I don't find the time to do this, my time will be wasted on things that aren't nearly as important.

Belinda.   So, when are you going to be a career artist?

Reno.   *(laughing)* Well, that's a dream, isn't it? If ever, it'll be a long time. Bills come first. Food, rent, transportation, yearly shots.

Wade.   *(on the radio)* Hello, my lovely passengers.

Belinda.   Uh, no. Don't tell me.

Reno.   Yeah, I had it on.

Wade.   This is the Midnight Sailor. We've just finished a lengthy set, and I do mean lengthy, of music to breath by, to cuddle to, even to soak in a hot bath to. It's time to take a few calls.

Belinda.   Can we just turn it off for a while?

Reno.   In a minute.

Belinda drinks some more.

Wade. Caller #1, you're on the air.

Caller #1. Midnight, I need some advice. My boyfriend and I have been dating for over a year. I thought he was the real deal, but I have just found out that he has not been as faithful to me as I have been to him.

Wade. Caller, what may I call you?

Caller #1. Jessie.

Wade. Okay, Jessie. You said that he has not been *as* faithful as you have? Does that leave room for the assumption that you have not been 100% loyal yourself?

Caller #1. Well, I am not perfect, no. But . . .

Wade. Well, Jessie. None of us are.

Belinda. Heaven help us. *(She drinks some more.)*

Wade. It seems to me that since neither of you are perfect or have been completely faithful, that you should not really be all that upset with him now.

Caller #1. But I have tried hard for several months. His is recent.

Wade. Well, again. Time heals all wounds. Maybe you could, in your own way, show him that he is not the only one who can do as he pleases.

Caller #1. Yeah, I'm listening . . .

Wade. If he knows you are always there and that he is your sole source of affection and attention, he may never come around. On the other hand, if he knows that you, being an attractive, independent woman, can find your own source of comfort apart from him, that may make a world of difference.

Caller #1. Yeah.

Belinda. What a crock!

Wade. I'll tell you what. we have to take a short break. Jessie, if you'll stay on the line for a while, I'll be right with you. *(Some sort of music or commercials begin.)*

Reno. Could you turn that off, Yago.

Yago.   Sure thing. *(He turns the radio off.)*

Belinda.   He did it again.

Reno.   *(Laughs.)* He is without a doubt the master.

Yago.   Lucky, lucky, lucky. The job with benefits.

Belinda.   Don't admire that in front of me. Please. *(She holds her head at her temples.)* Whew! You know, right this second, I am so drunk. It has definitely hit me. It slapped me in the face here. I'm officially toasted. This stuff is tough, Rembrandt!

Yago.   I've never seen her not in total control of her senses. How weird.

Belinda.   Don't count your chickens. I'm control, in I am, Yago.

Reno.   So, what are you up to tonight, Yago? Any exciting plans?

Yago.   Nah. Just came to check on you. I guess I'll just go home. Sleep. I don't have to be at the café until 2 tomorrow, so I can sleep in. Saturday bliss.

Reno.   Tomorrow's Saturday? I'd almost forgotten.

Yago.   Yes, it is. I might have to work on Saturdays, but I still have childhood fondness for them. I loved them. I guess I made it through the week because I knew they were coming. I didn't sleep in then. *(He laughs.)* Silly. I got up even earlier than I did on the other days. It wasn't as hard then. It was something I wanted to do. That's human nature, isn't it?

Reno.   Yeah.

Belinda snores lightly for a few seconds. They look at her—Yago continues.

Yago.   I got up and played outside with my friends. On most Saturdays, that was it. play, play, play. My mom would have to make me come in. I'd have to take a bath even to eat. That was most Saturdays. Other times, we'd go to my grandma's or my aunt's. It depended upon the days my dad was off work. We had so much fun on that block. I even kissed a girl right in front of my house. I kissed a girl, Reno. I was only eight, maybe nine.

Reno.   On a Saturday?

Yago.   *(smiling)* Yeah, must-a been. Okay, enough memory crap. Yeah, I'm sleeping in tomorrow. 'Til almost noon if I can get away with it.

Reno. So, is that what tomorrow brings? *(evidently in a much more philosophical mood than Yago)*

Yago. What? *(confused)*

Reno. Sleep. Is that what tomorrow brings?

Yago. Well, yeah. For me. For a little while. *(He laughs.)* What do you mean, Reno?

Reno. Nothing, Yago. Just me being silly.

Yago. Are you okay? If you need anything . . .

Reno. I'm fine, Yago. I'm good. Real good. In fact, I think I may be able to get some sleep in a little while. I'm about drawn-out tonight. I'm gonna read a little and go to bed.

Yago. Well, I'll take that as my cue to go. I'm gonna stop by O'Malley's.

Reno. I thought you were going home?

Yago. I am, eventually. A short detour doesn't count.

Reno. A short detour doesn't count?

Yago. Reno, are you okay. You're repeating me.

Reno. Go, Yag'. Have fun. Beware of people. They're the most dangerous thing out there.

Yago. Sleep, Reno. I'm going to seek out intelligent life. *(He starts to leave.)* If there is any. *(He looks at the sleeping Belinda.)* You've got quite some caretaker there.

Reno. Don't underestimate the . . . *(pauses and grins)* tigress.

Yago. Don't worry. I don't. Take care.

Yago leaves.

Reno. You, too. *(He locks the door behind Yago. He shuffles around a bit more—picks up a small mirror and talks to his reflection.)* You, too.

Reno picks up his blanket, picks up a book, sits on the floor, leans against a piece of furniture, and begins to read. In no time, he is asleep.

Scene 4

It is Reno's living room again. Several hours have passed. It is now Saturday morning. Reno is crumpled in a ball, asleep on the floor. Belinda is also asleep, but in a very uncomfortable-looking, contorted position. Her hair is extremely "messed up."

There is a series of very fast, very loud knocks on the door.

Belinda.   *(loud—still dreaming)* But, Mr. President . . . *(She laughs.)*

Reno screams in his sleep. Belinda is awakened immediately. The knocking continues.

Belinda.   What? What? *(Awakening)* Reno! *(She goes to him.)* Reno! Are you okay?

Reno.   Huh? No, I won't. *(Waking up)* Huh? Belinda?

Belinda.   Are you okay, sugar?

Reno.   Uh, yeah. *(He rubs his head.)* Is it morning already? The incessant pounding.

Belinda.   That's the door. *(She goes to answer it—and cracks it to see who is there.)* Annie?

Annie.   Belinda, you're here? I was wondering where you'd sneaked off to. *(She rushes in, in a nervous fashion.)*

Belinda.   I'm here, tending to Reno. Well, he won't let me. I'm keeping him company.

Annie.   Reno, how are you? I tried to stop by last night, but you know.

Reno.   I know. I'm fine.

Annie.   I really, really need to use your ladies' room. Really, really badly.

Reno.   Oh, okay.

Annie.   That's not the main reason I stopped. I wanted to check on you, but, . . . well, can I use it?

Reno.   It's more of a men's room, but yeah. Through there and to the left. Remember?

Annie.   *(Running)* Gotcha. *(Exits.)*

Reno.   When I'm well, nobody gives a flying flip. Let me get sick, and my living room becomes a regular waiting room.

Belinda.   People do give a flying flip. You just see it more when this happens. Whatever this is. I still don't know exactly what you had done. You've never . . .

Reno.   I could use some coffee. I think I'll go get me a cup. Care for any?

Belinda.   *(Slowly)* No. I'm fine. I may get some in a little while. Is it instant?

Reno.   Today it is. *(He starts to leave.)*

Belinda.   Yeah, bring me a cup. I could use a little pick-me-up. I think I have a crick in my neck. Your chair is not the most comfortable bed.

Reno.   Two cups. I'll be right back. *(He exits.)*

Belinda.   Okay. *(after he leaves)* You're elusive, my little spider. Very elusive. Not very good at it, though.

There is a knock at the door. Belinda, without thinking about it, goes to the door and opens it wide. Standing in the door, like a portrait, are three people. Nina, a middle-aged woman apparently trying to look a bit more upper-class than she actually is, Harold, a middle-aged pudgy man in a knit, pull-over shirt, and Marie, an elderly woman dressed strangely and wearing a full smile. She has the early stages of senile dementia and says maybe random things that the playwright hopes are perceived as humorous.

Belinda.   *(evidently not knowing these people)* Uh, hello.

Nina.   *(in a Southern, Georgia accent)* Well, hello, yourself, young lady.

Marie.   Cheerio!

Belinda.   Is there something I can do for you?

Nina.   I most certainly hope so. I do hope we have made our arrival at the correct abode?

Belinda.   Abode?

Nina.   It means *house*, darling.

Belinda.   I know it means . . .

Nina.   Is my son home?

Belinda.   Your son?

Reno re-enters the room. He has put on a shirt now and carries a can of whipped cream.

Reno.   I was out of instant. I'm having to make the real stuff. I found some whipped cream so we can turn them into cappuccinos and . . . *(He notices the visitors and drops the can.)*

Nina.   Reno!

Belinda.   Reno, you have visitors.

Reno stares dumbfounded.

Nina.   Reno! Reno! *(She steps forward.)* Ain't you gonna say anything?

Marie.   Trick or Treat.

Harold.   *(in a NON-Southern accent)* Momma, please. This isn't the time.

Nina.   *(holding out her arms excitedly)* So?!?!?

Belinda.   *(to Reno)* Are you going to say anything, Silly?

Reno.   *(searching)* Mom. What are you doing here?

Nina.   *(grabbing him)* What am I doing here? What am *I* doing here? What kind of question is that?

Reno.   A legitimate one.

Nina.   Reno Sunset Brooks!

Reno.   Don't use my . . .

Belinda.   Sunset?

35

Nina.	Of course, Sunset. You haven't told her that story?
Reno.	No, Mom. Now why are you here?
Nina.	There goes that question again. Son, son, son, that's enough to offend a mother. We heard that you were sick, had gone in the hospital for an operation . . .
Reno.	God help me.
Nina.	You look good. You had an operation. You're walking around just dandy.
Reno.	Who told you?
Harold.	Your sister.
Reno.	My sister I haven't seen in *years*? How . . .
Nina.	It's called email, Reno. Internet. It's the stuff of the future.
Reno.	I do that *stuff* for a living.
Harold.	That sounds intriguing, Reno. Remarkably intriguing. *(He smiles a smile that matches his mother's.)*
Reno.	An email from who?? And what's he *(pointing to Harold)* doing here, Mother?
Nina.	First, an email from that Casanova friend of yours. That radio stud. What's his name?
Belinda.	Wade?
Nina.	Yeah, that's it. Wade. He emailed Annabelle Lee and told her, and she called me. It's amazing that she caught me—considering that we were on our honeymoon—which leads me to your second question. Come here, Harold. *(He joins her and holds her hand.)* Harold and I just married. You remember Harold, don't you?
Reno.	Yeah, hi, Harold.
Harold.	Hi, Reno.
Reno.	I thought you two divorced a few years ago. What happened to Milo Milner?

Nina.   Oh, time does fly, Sweetie. Milo died before our first anniversary. He went to the john when we were on a flight to Vancouver. I wondered what was talking him so long. I knew supper had been real spicy, but after he was in there a long time, long enough for me to get through eleven chapters of *The Lust of the Savage Heart*, a classy romance novel by Esmerelda Dubose, I just love her books, I started to get worried. I asked one of those male stewardesses, well, flight attendants, or whatever the hell they call them, to go check on Milo, and he was sitting there on the throne like Elvis incarnate. He had one of those prearranged funeral packages, and he wanted to be burned and dumped out over Lake Erie, for some unknown reason—I don't know if they actually did that with the crumbs or not, but, anyway, the prearrangement funeral plan man was helping me into the slab house, and he asked me out. Can you believe that? Milo wasn't even in the oven yet, and this tall, handsome, well, somewhat handsome, except for that overbite, anyway, this tall gentleman asks me to dinner. I was so distraught and lonely, I accepted. We were married later that month. I was Mrs. Nina Sizemore. That didn't last too long. I found out that he was sleeping around with the florist lady who provided most of the flowers for Milo's service, well, it was actually more of a wake, but I'm not going to go into that. Needless to say, I was royally ticked off. I mean, I can handle quite a bit, but I ain't gonna tolerate anybody cheating on me.

Marie.   Cheating!

Harold.   Momma.

Nina.   I was at Rudy Gibaltee's, a little bistro not far from where me and Clarence—that was the funeral man's name, Clarence Sizemore—where we lived. And in walks Harold. I thought, "Is that Harold?" And I then I saw Marie, you remember Harold's mother . . . ?

Reno.   Yeah.

Nina.   And I knew it was him. He saw that I was crying. They came over, and the rest is history. I divorced Clarence and accepted Harold's invitation to remarry me—all because he walked up to me.

Harold.   I couldn't help. I love this woman.

Nina.   And I love you, Sugar Dumpling.

Marie.   Love is a many splendored thing.

Reno.   But you were divorced, like, three marriages back.

Harold. I was foolish to have left your mother. I was really confused. There were issues that I had trouble with.

Nina. Yeah, but he figured out his true orientation and knows that he loves me.

Marie. Orientation is a many splendored thing.

Harold. Momma.

Reno. So, you're Mrs. Greene again. *Greene*, is that right?

Nina. Yeah.

Harold. Right-o, my little pal.

Reno. So, this is number . . . *(leading)*

Nina. Oh, Reno, please!

Reno. No, seriously. That's, uh, that's *ten* now, isn't it?

Nina. Some of those don't count.

Reno. But it's ten.

Nina. Yes, Mr. Brooks—your father. Ed Marcus. Kozlowski. Baker—that wasn't but a year either. Goldberg. Gonzales—he was so cute . . . sorry, Harold. Harold here *(patting him and smiling)*. Milner. Sizemore. And now Greene again. That does make ten, doesn't it? Makes quite a signature. *(She laughs.)* But I am very content with Greene again. I know this is right.

Reno. I'm sure you do.

Nina. So, tell me about this operation. I had to come see my baby doll.

Reno. I'm not your baby doll.

Annie re-enters from the bathroom.

Annie. Sorry I took so long. Reno, you have some great magazines in there. I couldn't stop reading. Oh, I'm sorry. I didn't mean to interrupt.

Belinda. You're missing the fun.

Nina.   Reno, I was about to ask you the name of this nice young lady that you so rudely failed to introduce me to. But now I have to ask you to introduce me to these *two* young ladies.

Harold.   Yes, Reno, introduce them.

Marie.   Two and one make three!

Reno.   You've actually met them. You just don't remember. It was four years ago, the last time I saw or heard from you.

Nina.   Such is life dear.

Belinda.   I'm Belinda.

Annie.   And I'm Annie.

Nina.   Aw, such a lovely name. I have a daughter named Annabelle Lee. She's the light of my life.

Annie.   Annabelle Lee. How interesting.

Nina.   Yes, me and her father, Artie Kozlowski, God rest his soul, were vacationing in Monaco. That's where she was conceived. So, I named her Annabelle Lee because we made her in a kingdom by the sea.

Marie.   Many and many a year ago, in this kingdom by the sea, . . . we loved with a love that was more that love . . . ahh . . .

Nina.   Growing up, I knew a girl named Canoe, because her folks conceived her in a canoe on the Chattahoochee, and I always swore I'd name my kids after the place where love spawned them.

Belinda and Annie look at Reno.

Reno.   Shut up. *(He walks to the other side of the room.)*

Belinda.   Reno Sunset Brooks.

Annie.   Sunset?

Nina.   And what a sunset that was. It was our honeymoon in Nevada.

Harold.   Nina, that really hurts me when you talk about your past love joy-joys.

Annie.   *Love joy-joys?*

Marie. Lovin' on borrowed time.

Nina. I'm so sorry, Harold. I forgot.

Reno. And this is my mom's tenth husband . . .

Annie. Tenth? *(Laughs.)* Come on, Reno. That's cruel.

Belinda. Annie . . .

Annie. *(Continuing)* And that's not like you. You're one of the only non-cruel men I know.

Belinda. Annie . . .

Annie. Tenth. I'm ashamed of you.

Belinda. Annie!

Annie. What?

Belinda. It *is* the tenth.

Annie. What?

Reno. As I was saying, may I introduce you to my mother's tenth husband, Harold Greene. He was actually my step father years ago—for a while.

Harold. You ladies are charming. Love your hair.

Marie. Unsightly hairs? Laser removal work wonders.

Reno. And this is Harold's mother, Marie Greene. This was indeed one of the ones that I truly liked. She's a sweet lady.

Harold. She's getting a little old, losing touch with reality, if you know what I mean.

Belinda. *(to Marie)* Mrs. Greene.

Marie. I am Marie, Marie, Marie.

Belinda. It's nice to meet you, Marie.

Marie. You want some advice, Eva Gabor?

Belinda.   Um, sure.

Marie.   Sweetie, you can lead a fish to water, but you can't make him swim—unless you beat the tarnation out of him. That always works wonders.

Belinda.   Thank you. I'll remember that.

Nina.   And who *are* these two beautiful young ladies, Reno?

Reno.   They are my friends, Mother.

Nina.   Female friends. How sheik. How modern. Very 21st Century. Did I meet you two at the wedding?

Belinda.   Yes.

Annie.   Yeah, I remember. You did.

Reno.   That was the last time I saw you, myself.

Nina.   Life is tough, dear. Be thankful. I did come to your wedding.

Reno.   I didn't have a wedding.

Nina.   Well, you almost did. It wasn't the wedding that was missing. It was the bride.

Reno.   Thank you. Thank you, Mom.

Nina.   Oh, Reno. You should have known she wouldn't show up.

Reno.   What? How would you know that? You never met her.

Nina.   I saw her picture that day. You can tell a lot about a picture. The eyes. The eyes say it all. She was man hopper. Plain and simple.

Belinda.   Got any more of that alcohol, Sunset?

Nina.   Don't tell me you drink, Reno! That's stuff's bad news. That's what killed my Ed Marcus—remember?

Reno.   No, it's for medicinal purposes only.

Nina.   Good.

Harold.   That's wise decision-making, Reno. Alcohol, although bad for recreational uses, a major inhibitor of responses and clear thinking, is an ideal choice for healthy body function.

Reno.   Thank you, Harold.

Harold.   You're welcome.

Marie.   Hooch makes a person regular.

Harold.   Thank you, Momma. That is so true.

Annie.   How much you got, Reno?

Reno.   Not enough.

Nina.   Back to the surgery. What was wrong?

Reno.   Nothing, Mom.

Nina.   They don't do surgery for nothing. I know that. Oh, I forgot to tell you. I had all the plumbing pulled out. Don't look for that little brother you always wanted.

Reno.   Thanks for the information, Mom. I'll mark that off my nightly prayers.

Marie.   Father, bless me for I have sinned. It has been sixty-three years since my last confession.

Harold.   Momma, we're not in church.

Marie.   I know. Smells like a brewery in here. Where's the juice?

Nina.   What was the operation??

Reno.   Forget it, Mom. I'm okay.

Nina.   I'm a mother. I don't forget nothing. What was it?

Reno.   Mom, it's been four years, four years, and you show up because of an email my best friend sent my sister whom I've not seen in a longer time . . .

Annie.   Wade sent your sister an email?

Reno. *(continuing)* And you show up? Just show up with Harold Greene? And don't get me wrong, Harold. You're a nice guy. But you show up and want to know about a hospital stay?

Nina. Yes. Tell me.

Annie. Is your sister married?

Reno. I don't know. Is Annabelle Lee married?

Nina. No.

Reno. *(to Annie)* No, she's not.

Nina. She was almost, but her finance' fell off a horse and broke his neck.

Annie. Hmm. Oh, okay.

Marie. You gotta show a horse who's boss. Sometimes, he forgets and tells all his friends that he's in control. You can't let that happen. Society would be in shambles.

Nina. The operation?

Reno. It was nothing, Mom.

Nina. It was something.

Reno. No, it was nothing. I'm waiting to hear about . . . *(stops)*

Nina. Waiting to hear what?

Belinda. Waiting?

Marie. Poor Godot.

Reno. Look, I'm fine. I'm a grown man. I have taken care of myself for a long time, a very long time.

Nina. Listen . . .

Reno. No. I'm tired of the games. I've played them. I played them all over. I became Mr. Responsibility with Grandma while you surfed the world over.

Nina. Reno.

Reno.   No, wait. I sat and watched her die. And I don't regret it. Not a bit. She had me there. And I was there. Every day. I did my best. Games. I've had some doozies for friends, and lost them, thankfully, and I do have some decent friends now . . .finally. Some of us are going on seven, eight, ten years. And then I fall in love with Jaclyn, yes, shifty-eyes Jaclyn. And she decides to not show up at what's supposed to be the most important day of our lives. And I never, never hear from her again. I hear by rumor that she moved to Kentucky or Ohio or somewhere.

Nina.   It was Indiana.

Reno.   How do you know?

Nina.   You're sister's an encyclopedia of facts.

Reno.   Annabelle Lee knows? She doesn't even know her. Hell, she barely knows me.

Nina.   Go on, dear. Let it all out.

Reno.   (*Loudly*) Ugh!!!

Marie.   Screaming is essential. Keeps the bears away.

Reno.   I sink myself into my job. Programming, typing, programming, staring at a soul-draining monitor all day.

Nina.   Please tell me you're dating again.

Reno just stares at her.

Belinda.   Touchy subject. Let's not go there.

Nina.   Please tell me that you're still not over the girl with the shifty eyes.

Harold.   You gotta move on, Reno. Loving is good for you. Keeps you healthy.

Marie.   Hooch and canoodling. Does a body good.

Nina.   Thank you, Marie.

Reno.   And I have one or two things that keep me going. One or two lights that shine, and . . . . (*He gets a little emotional.*) And then, yes, I have some personal health problems. (*He straightens up and speaks with authority.*) And I like that word. Personal. (*He exits to the other part of the house.*)

Nina.   Should somebody go after him?

Harold.   Let him be. A man needs a good cry at least once a day.

Nina.   Well, I need a good smoke. You girls got something stronger than my cigs?

Belinda and Annie look at each other in disbelief.

Belinda and Annie. (*Slowly*) No.

Nina.   You should look into it. A year in Amsterdam teaches you so much.

At that point, Wade knocks on the door and comes on it the house. He is in running clothes and is hot and sweaty.

Wade.   Hey, everybody. How's Picasso today?

Nina.   If it's not the radio stud!

Marie.   Hubba. Hubba.

Wade.   Oh, Mrs. . . . Mrs. . . . Well, Reno's mom.

Nina.   Greene. It's Greene, Radio Stud.

Belinda.   It's Wade. Just plain Wade.

Wade.   It's nice to see you again. It's been quite some time since . . .

Nina.   We've been through that, Stud. All through that. We came to check on Reno, who seems to be quite well, or at least well enough to storm out of here mad at me.

Wade.   Yeah, he's got a lot . . .

Nina.   On his mind. We know. Anyway, thanks for keeping Annabelle Lee informed.

Annie.   Yeah, I'm sure Annabelle Lee is appreciative of your email, Wade. Very appreciative.

Wade.   Well, I figured she should know about him being sick and all. I mean— she is his sister and . . .

Nina. And she can tell me. Albeit, I am hard to track down, but Annabelle Lee can usually guess where I am. She's psychic, you know.

Belinda. No, I didn't know.

Nina. She only does that on the side. She runs a singles' club in Philadelphia now.

Wade. I had her email. I thought she should know.

Harold. That was very kind of you, Radio Stud.

Annie. It's Wade.

Nina. This is my new, well, yeah . . . this is Harold. I'm married to him. And that's his mother. I'm going to smoke.

Nina walks outside.

Wade. Harold. Harold's mother.

Nina walks back in. She holds her cigarette out the door as she talks.

Nina. You called him Picasso. Is he still painting?

Wade. Look. They're everywhere.

Nina. (*Looks.*) Oh, they are. Hmm. (*She goes back outside.*)

Marie. The women come and go, talking of Michelangelo.

Harold. I don't understand art.   *(He walks around looking at the paintings)* I don't get these pictures, even. People just spend hours putting color on color. I don't get it.

Belinda. It's just art, Mr. Greene. And Reno is very good at it.

Harold. I still don't get it.

Wade. It's a means of expression.

Annie. Like email?

Wade. No, that's communication. There's a big difference.

Belinda.   Speaking of communication, what happened with Caller #1, Ms. Jessie, last night?

Wade.   Two nights in row? I have a fan.

Belinda.   Calm down, Juan. Reno and Yago were listening. I overheard. So, did you end up visiting a lonely Jessie this morning?

Annie.   I gotta go. I have an appointment at the salon in a few minutes. (*She leaves abruptly.*)

Belinda.   So, did you?

Wade.   That's for me to know—and you never to find out.

Harold.   (*looking at a painting*) What is this supposed to be? A house or something?

Belinda.   I believe that's a woman sitting in a field.

Harold.   This gives me a headache, a big headache. Whew. I'm going to check on Nina. Can you two watch Momma for a minute?

Belinda.   Watch Momma?

Harold.   Thanks, doll. *(He exits.)*

Wade.   Thanks, doll.

Marie.   Aren't we the ragamuffin crew?

Belinda.   Something like that.

Wade.   Cheer up, Belinda.

Marie.   Yeah, cheer up, *mon chéri*. Things are not always as they seem.

Wade.   That's the honest truth.

Marie.   In fact, things are seldom as they seem.

Belinda.   You're suddenly coherent.

Marie.   Coherence is appearance.

Wade.   A poet.

Marie.   Mother Goose took a lover once, Radio Stud.

Belinda.   Okay, I take that back.

The phone rings again. Belinda answers it.

Belinda.   Hello. Oh. Yago . . . yeah. You don't wanna know. Seriously. Well, his mom showed up with . . . Yeah, me either. Exactly. Four years. Since the wedding, well, what was to be the wedding. No, they're outside. No, I think he's in his bedroom, or taking a bath. I'll tell you later. Okay, what? I don't know. I'll ask. I don't know if I can, but I'll ask him. If I can't, I'll see if Wade wants to. Okay. That's fine. Okay. Yeah, you, too. Bye, wine boy.

Wade.   If Wade wants to what?

Belinda.   Get Reno out of the house. Yago wants to buy him a special dinner down at the diner. He's just worried about him.

Wade.   We'll see.

Belinda.   I know.

Marie.   Four years since the wedding. Four years.

Belinda.   Yes, four. The wedding that never was. Shhh, Marie. That's sorta painful for Reno.

Marie.   And when is your wedding.

Belinda.   (*Laughs.*) Not again for a long time. I'm still trying to get over my first trip down the aisle.

Marie.   Ah, you baked the cake once before?

Belinda.   Uh, yeah. For a few months. But he had other cake on the side.

Marie.   The bakery is full of tempting treats. pies, cakes, donuts, sweet breads, cinnamon rolls, jelly rolls . . .

Wade.   Okay, I'm getting hungry.

Belinda.   Cad.

Wade.   For real sweets, Belinda. The metaphor's outstretched its limits.

Marie.   Oh, I was married. I married once, and that was all. Hiram Mordechai Greene. He died one night while I slept. A great tragedy. Caught me off-guard.

Belinda.   I'm sorry.

Marie.   Greene. Greene. Greene. His lips were not the first, though. No, sir-ree, not at all. I was fifteen the first time I kissed a boy. His name was Oscar. His daddy was a store owner, clothing, fine apparel, fit for the city woman. Oscar's lips were sweet, like plums. Honestly, better than plums. Like liquid sugar. He was handsome young man, thick arms, broad chest, flat stomach, cute little belly button . . .

Wade.   It's good to see you have memories, Mrs. Greene.

Marie.   Mrs. Greene. No. Mrs. Greene was Hiram's mother. I'm Marie. Call me "Marie." Marie is me. Lovely Oscar. Lovely, lovely learned boy. My tender poet, my wise little scholar. And what a voice. He read me Shakespeare. And Browning. And Marlowe. And . . . yes, Matthew Arnold, "Dover Beach,".

> "The sea is calm to-night.
> The tide is full, the moon lies fair
> Upon the straits;--on the French coast, the light
> Gleams and is gone; the cliffs of England stand,
> Glimmering and vast, out in the tranquil bay.
> Come to the window, sweet is the night-air!"

Yes, he read me poetry. That was his gift to me. *(Weak, she looks up teary-eyed and pretends to pluck imaginary fruit out the air—as if taking his gifts.)*

Belinda.   *(Gently)* And then you met Hiram?

Marie.   Hiram. He couldn't kiss worth a hoot. And his breath stank like turnips. He couldn't help it, though. He tried. Ate peppermints like they were free. Never any good. Hell-atosis. He was a good man. Worked hard. Loved hard. Tried hard. It don't matter, though, how things work out. What matters is . . . if we've tried.

Reno walks in, wearing a robe.

Reno.   Babysitting?

Belinda.   Listening.

Marie.   There a sweet pea!

Reno.   Oh, Marie. (*He hugs her.*) You *were* always the sweetheart.

Marie.   I'm a vixen in disguise.

Wade.   I believe her.

Nina and Harold reenter.

Nina.   I see you're back.

Reno.   I see you're back, too.

Nina.   I don't know what's going on, if you're waiting on some sort of test results or what, and I know you're upset about a whole passel of things, so, me and Harold, and Marie, unless you want her, are going to a hotel downtown. You need some time to cool off and figure out what you want or need. We need to eat and sleep. We'll let you know where we are. I intend on knowing what's wrong. You *are* my son.

Reno just stands there, his arms folded.

Nina.   Are you ready, Marie?

Marie.   Elvis has left the building. You know, his hips were always so strong-looking.

Nina.   Reno, we're going. I'll see you soon. Okay?

He stands there.

Nina.   Okay?

Reno.   Okay.

Nina.   Okay.

Harold.   Nina, carry Momma to the car. I need to talk to Reno for a second.

Nina.   What?

Harold.   I'll be there in a second, my love.

Nina and Marie walk out the door.

Marie.   (*leaving*) Too many cooks make a dish way too seasoned, my friends.

Harold.   Reno, I know things are confusing to you right now. Your mom is not the most normal woman in the world, but she's a good lady. She's good to me. And you got this sickness thing going on that you don't wanna tell us about, and that's okay. You're grown. You can take care of yourself. And that shifty-eyes girl dumping you four years ago. I don't have anything to say about that, but I do want to say this. You've had a few step-fathers, well, close to a dozen I know, and I was one once before. But I wasn't a good one. I just want you to know . . . you know that I ain't got no kids of my own and I won't never. But I wanna be a father to you. I don't understand you one little bit. I know you like all this art and drawing crap. Personally, I think it's a big waste of time, but like I said, you're grown, big enough to make your own screw-ups. That happened until you find what it is in life you need to do. I tell ya. I wouldn't know what to do if I didn't sell meat. Meat's my life. Sausage, ham, steaks, roasts, you name it. Meat's made me a lot of dough. But that's me. Yeah, get you a woman. You need one. It's not good for a man to be a loner. You need to relax and just . . . live. Okay enough talk. Back to what I was saying. You need a dad. I can be one. When you decide, let me know. (*He hugs a stunned Reno and leaves.*)

Reno collapses and stares at Belinda and Wade.

Belinda.   Wanna go to Max's later? Yago's buying.

Reno.   He works there. He gets everything at half-price.

Belinda.   Like I said, Yago's buying.

Reno.   I don't know. If I feel like it.

Belinda.   I feel like I've been to a strange movie.

Reno.   Welcome to my world.

Belinda.   I'm going home. I need a hot bath. And no, don't offer yours. I want my own.

Reno.   I wasn't going to offer.

Belinda.   Good. I'll call in a couple of hours. Decide by then, or I may do something else.

Reno.   Okay. Thanks for staying with me.

Belinda.   For you, anything. *(She gives him a fast kiss on the mouth.)* Ciao, compadres. *(to Wade)* See you a little later, Radio Stud. *(She leaves.)*

Wade.   *(picking up a book, but not reading)* Four years, huh?

Reno.   Don't, Wade.

Wade.   Don't "don't" to me.   This is Wade. *(starting again)* Four years, huh?

Reno.   *(A deep audible breath)* Yeah. Four years. This month.

Wade.   Hmm. That sucks.

Reno.   Yeah.

Wade.   And next year, it'll be five, then six, then seven. Every day of the rest of your life will always be a number. It'll *always* be a marker. Always. Always. Six years, two months. Eight years, seven months, twelve days. Twenty-three years, four months, two weeks, six days, and five hours. Always.

Reno.   *(Sits quietly for a little while and then speaks)* Are you finished with the numbers?

Wade.   Yeah.

Reno.   You take care of Caller #1 last night?

Wade.   When did I become Mr. Popularity Show?

Reno.   You're my best friend.   I know you.

Wade.   I told her to forgive him.

Reno.   And . . .

Wade.   And nothing.   I told her to forgive him. And I gave her two free tickets to some concert the station's promoting.

Reno.   That's it?

Wade.   That's it.

Reno.   So, what'd you do last night after work then?

Wade.   My turn. You mom freaked you out, huh?

Reno.   Wade, she's never around, going through the phone book, hunting for men
              . . .

Wade.   No, not that. I know that's all freaky. I mean her probing.

Reno.   Probing?

Wade.   The surgery. All that. Trying to get you to tell her what you are keeping to
              yourself.

Reno.   Wade . . .

Wade.   Buddy, I'm not asking. I don't ask when I know you don't wanna tell. It's
              a sorta don't ask, don't tell thing. Well, no, not really.

Reno.   Not really.

Wade.   But I'm telling you. I'm here if you need to tell. Some things, you gotta
              figure out. Sometimes even the quiet of a dark empty bedroom, with
              nothing but a blanket, a pillow, a ceiling to stare at. Other times, you need
              an ear. And for the record, I've got two.

Reno hugs Wade.

Reno.   Thanks, Wade. I'm just really scared.

Wade.   I know. Well, I don't know, but you know . . . I know.

Reno.   I know.

Wade.   You need to get dressed. We're stopping by my place so that I can get
              cleaned up and then, we're all going to Max's tonight. Yago's buying.
              Your meal at least.

Reno.   I don't know.

Wade.   I know. Go get dressed. You look like a stripper.

Reno shakes his hips as he gets up. They laugh. He stops and looks at a painting.

Wade.   And that'll take off.

Reno.   I don't care if it takes off. It's just important. As it is.

Wade.   I know. But it'll take off. Passions aren't complete until they consume you. You're remarkably good. Some of us even realize it in your lifetime. You're lucky. Now go get dressed, Picasso.

Reno touches the painting and exits. Wade goes to the painting and touches it, too. He looks to the place where Reno made his exit, refocuses on the painting, touches it again, and walks back to a chair, sits, and leans his head back.

Scene 5

Max's. The meal is over. Reno, Wade, Belinda, Annie, and Yago are talking and laughing. They are dressed very nicely.

Yago.   And then I told him that I didn't have time for that. His face turned a shade of red, and he just turned around and walked off.

They all laugh.

Wade.   Yago, you are indeed the strangest fellow I know.

Yago.   Why thank you, my dear Wade. *(He leans toward Wade.)*

Wade.   Watch it, Yago. You're leaning.

Yago.   You notice. Perception is alive and well.

Belinda.   I can't believe that we haven't argued one bit tonight. I am shocked.

Reno.   Not nearly as shocked as I am.

Wade.   It's actually a pleasant evening, a fun one. Just here.

Yago.   We should go dancing.

Reno.   Have at it. I'm going home when I leave here. I am still a bit tired.

Yago.   Still sore?

Reno.   I'm okay.

Belinda.   I'd love to dance. I haven't been in ages. Well, days are ages to some. *(She laughs.)*

Reno. Seriously. You guys go. Don't let me stop you.

Annie. We're not going out without you. Forget it.

Reno. No, that's not. . .

Annie. Quiet. You're overruled.

From across the room, a young lady walks up.

Zoe. Reno?

Reno. Hey. Oh, hey. How are you?

Zoe. Good, I thought that was you over here. How are you? We're all worried about you, and we haven't heard a thing.

Reno. Zoe, these are my friends, Wade, Belinda, Yago, Annie. Guys, this is Zoe. She works in the same office with me. She just got assigned in there with the old guys.

Zoe. Don't be silly. Old in that room is young anywhere else. *(to the friends)* Hello. It's nice to meet you all.

They say hello to her.

Zoe. So, are you okay?

Reno. Yeah, I'm fine. Things are good.

Zoe. So, your operation went okay?

Reno. Yeah, fine and dandy. Everything is fine. And dandy.

Zoe. That is good to hear.

Reno. Would you like to join us?

Zoe. Well, to be honest, I am here with my brother and his fiancée. *(She points and laughs.)* Remember him?

Reno. Yeah. *(Reno and Zoe both wave toward offstage.)*

Zoe. We just ordered.

Wade.   Well, go tell them you're going to sit with us a minute.

Zoe.   Well, I hate to intrude.

Reno.   It's no intrusion.

Zoe.   Okay. Hold on. (*She runs off.*)

Belinda.   Well, what was that, Wade?

Wade.   Couldn't you tell she wanted to come and sit with Reno?

Reno.   What?

Annie.   Yes, I noticed.

Reno.   You guys are crazy. She's a friend.

Wade.   Okay, she's a friend, then.

Reno.   You guys are amazing.

Belinda.   Reno, she's cute. She seems sweet, too.

Reno.   I work with her.

Yago.   Yeah, she's cute. She's not my type, of course, but she is cute. Now, back at her table . . .

Annie.   Hush, wine-o.

Reno.   She's just so happy and vibrant . . . You don't really think . . .?

Belinda.   Hush. Here she comes.

Zoe.   Hey. I told them I was going to sit over here a little while. They're cool with that.

Wade.   Great. Pull up a chair.

Zoe sits.

Zoe.   So, what are you all up to tonight? Good friends, good food?

Annie.   Something like that.

Yago.   A little celebration over nothing really, getting Reno out of the house. Get him to finally put a shirt on. (Annie slaps his arms hard.) Ouch.

Wade.   We're just making sure Reno gets out of the house. He's had a lot on his mind.

Zoe.   Yeah, with the hospital and all. (to Reno) Are you sure you're doing fine?

Reno.   I'm good.

Zoe.   That's good to know. Because that office would be boring without you. I mean . . . Well, you know our jobs are not the most exciting in the world . . . no . . .

Reno.   I know what you mean, and thanks.

Belinda.   I was trying to get him to go dancing, but he doesn't feel like going out.

Zoe.   Oh, I can understand that.

Yago.   Wait!! *(He jumps up smiling and runs off.)*

Zoe.   Is something wrong?

ALL.   That's Yago.

Belinda.   Yago's quite the character.   And I think I know what he's doing.

Annie.   I'll bet money I know.

Wade.   Yep.

Reno.   Oh, Lord.

Music begins. It's slow to moderate paced, older pop music—maybe Sinatra or Sammy Davis, Jr., or jazz.

Yago runs back up.

Yago.   There's a stereo system under the counter. Not a radio. Just a CD player. And that's all we have. Sorry.

Belinda.   That's actually nice, Yago. Not exactly what I had in mind, but nice.

Zoe.   You're going to dance?

Yago.   Why not? (*to Belinda*) *Mad 'dam.*

Belinda.   *Monsieur.* (*She gets up, and they start to dance.*)

Reno.   (*to Zoe*) Are we embarrassing you?

Zoe.   Not in the least. Such is life.

Reno stares at her.

Zoe.   Did I say something wrong?

Reno.   No.

Wade.   (*to Zoe*) Care to join me? (*He holds out his hand to Zoe.*) Ms. Zoe?

Zoe.   (*takes his hand*) But of course.

Reno looks at Wade, who winks at him. Wade and Zoe dance.

Annie looks at Reno.

Annie.   I'm not a pity case.

Reno.   I am. I'm the sick one.

Annie.   (*stands up, smiles, and holds out her arms*) Come here.

Reno joins her and they start to dance.

Belinda.   This is sort of fun.

Wade.   The music's not bad, either.

Reno.   Not bad? It's great.

Yago.   And we're getting relatively few stares.

Annie.   You're blind, then.

Belinda.   I don't care.

Annie.   I don't either.

Wade.   The stares don't matter. It's the dance that counts.

They dance.

Zoe, very nicely breaks her dance with Wade, stands back, watches, and then cuts into the dance with Reno. Annie stands back while Zoe and Reno dance. Wade reaches his hand to Annie, who first looks at the others. Wade re-extends his hand as if to say, "Here." Annie takes it gently and they begin to dance a slow, romantic dance.

Zoe.   When I was a little girl, my grandfather danced with me. I'd stand on top of his feet and he's move for both of us. I learned rhythm that way. I learned to feel the moves, step by step.

Reno.   That's sweet.

Zoe.   You're a good dancer. Who taught you?

Reno.   I learned on my own. My dad died when I was too young to remember, and my mom wasn't there even when she was there.

Zoe.   I'm sorry.

Reno.   Don't be sorry. I'm over it.

Belinda.   Don't you believe it.

Reno.   Belinda.

Belinda.   Sorry.

Zoe.   You have a natural grace. God-given.

Wade.   We try to tell him that all the time.

Reno.   Can't a man have a conversation?

Yago.   Tonight, no.

Wade.   And you should see his art. He's a regular Van Gogh.

Reno.   Please! I thought I was Picasso.

Belinda.   And such humility.

Reno.   I . . .

Wade.   Let's shut up and dance.

They all dance for a while. Reno shows evidence of weakness—and stumbles a little.

Belinda.   You okay, Reno?

Annie.   Reno . . .

Reno.   Yeah. It's nothing.

Yago.   Nothing?

Reno.   Come on, guys. Shut up and dance.

They dance.

Reno stops and looks around.

Belinda.   What's wrong?

Reno.   I can't do this.

Wade.   What?

Reno.   I can't do this.

He walks off briskly. Wade follows.

Wade.   Reno.

Lights down.

Scene 6

Reno' s house. Thirty minutes later. Reno enters, followed by Wade and Belinda

Reno.   I can't do this.

Wade.   Can't do what? Live? Dance? I wish you'd answer me. That's all you've
said all the way from Max's. "I can't do this." Do what? Talk to me.

Belinda.   Come on, Reno.

Reno.   *(Kicking off his shoes and pulling off his socks as he walks)* Any of this. Don't you get it?

Reno pours himself and drink and swallows it in one shot.

Wade.   No, you won't let me. Tell me, Reno. If you didn't, I could understand. But it's gone beyond that now. This is not normal at all.

Belinda.   Reno, if you need to talk to Wade, I can wait outside for Annie and Yago.

Reno.   *(pulling off his shirt)* No, I can't talk.

Wade.   Reno . . . *(pauses)* okay. Don't then.

Belinda.   Don't?

Wade.   Don't. If he can't, he can't. But there are some things that are obvious. There are some facts here.

Reno.   And they are?

Wade.   One. there is more to this surgery thing than you've let on. And you're right. it is your business, but there is more. Two, that girl back there, Zoe? She likes you. I don't know what's going on in your head, but there was a girl back there who appears intelligent, and is pretty, and is sweeter that all of us put together, and she likes you, and I thought, just maybe from the dance, for a few minutes that you might like her a little. We are not eighteen anymore—or twenty-one. Heck, we're not even twenty-five. We're at the third way mark, my pouty friend, maybe half the rate we eat and drink sometimes. That's not something you run out and cry about like a little sissy.

Reno.   A little sissy? Is that what you think?

Wade.   And I say this because I love you. I don't have brother or a sister or anything like that, so I know a smidgeon how it feels to be you, just a smidgeon, but if you are going to pass up a possibility for a bit of happiness because a maladjusted, shallow coward stood you up at your wedding four years ago, you're a defeated man. You might as well hang up the sneakers now.

Belinda.   *(looking at Wade in respect and awe)* I'm in awe.

Reno.   You really think it's about *Jaclyn*?

Wade.   Yeah.

Reno.   You *do*?

Wade.   Yeah.

Reno.   (*to Belinda*) Do *you*?

Belinda.   I don't know *what* to think, darling.

Reno.   I have tried to be as vague as I can.   I'm there dancing with this Zoe, and I'm really liking it, but I realize I can't. And it has nothing to do with Jaclyn. Nothing.

Wade.   Then what? If not her, then what, Reno? What's going on here?

Reno.   (*fast, upset, almost hyperventilating the whole time*) What's going on here? Okay. You really want to know. Everybody wants to know. Okay. Wade. Belinda. I might as well tell you. There are no two people I trust more in the world. So, are you sure you want to know?

Wade.   We want to know. You're the most talented person I know. I love and respect you, but something's going on here.

Reno.   Okay. Watch closely. (*He faces them and rips off the bandage. There is no incision, no nothing underneath*) See this? (*He turns around and around.*)

Belinda.   I don't get it.

Wade.   You didn't have surgery at *all*?

Reno.   Oh, you wanted to know, right? Right? Still care to know?

Wade.   Yeah.

Reno faces away from the audience—and Wade and Belinda—and puts his hand on his head.

Reno.   So, my dearest friends. (*He turns around and holds his hands high in the air. It's obvious that this action exposes how sore he is.*)

Belinda.   (*Kindly, confused.*) What?

Reno brings his hands down and leaves them palms up at what would be the area of a belt buckle, near his . . . "man" region.

Wade.   Wait. Are you saying . . .?

Reno.   Yes, Wade. The ultimate low blow.

They are wide-eyed. Wade looks at Belinda, who holds her stare on Reno.

Belinda.   Reno, are you saying that you have . . .?

Reno.   What do you think? See what's on my mind. *(He turns away, hands on his head again.)*

Belinda.   *What* did . . .?

Wade.   What did you have to have done? Did you have surgery . . . there?

Reno.   So now I can tell? It's called testicular cancer. Ever heard of that? Hits you right where it counts, Wade, huh? Right here. *(He moves one hand near the "area.")*

Belinda.   Oh, baby . . .

Wade.   That's . . . Did they have to . . .?

Reno.   Yeah. They did. Singular removal.

Belinda.   Oh, baby . . . I'm sorry . . .

Wade.   But, wait. I heard that . . . I always thought that that was something that could be taken care of with no big problems. *(Pauses)* I'm getting the feeling that this is more intense than I had ever . . .

Reno.   I don't have a regular case. I have a bad one. It took a more radical incision.

Wade.   And . . . they . . . *(He tries to make an appropriate hand motion to refer to the surgery but stops before he embarrasses himself.)*

Reno.   Yeah. Gone, Wade. Pretty intense. I feel like a . . . child.

Belinda.   But that doesn't matter. You know, I've read that one is . . . well . . . plenty for . . . you know?

Reno.   Yeah, one is, but none's not.

Wade.   I don't understand.

Reno.   They did what they had to do. It was worst than they thought. They removed it. Then they saw that the other one may have problems, too. They just don't take all you have, (*crying*) your only chance for . . . they don't take everything with one fatal laugh unless they know that they . . . *know* that . . . it's beyond hope. That's the call I'm waiting for. They won't know until Monday.

Belinda.   (*Grabbing him*) Oh, Reno. I am so sorry. (*He starts to cry again.*)

Wade.   How did you . . . uh, get it?

Reno.   Well, it certainly wasn't from an abundance of romance. It's cancer, my friend. It's cancer.

Wade.   Why keep all this to yourself, man? (*He joins the hug, too.*)

Reno.   Think about it, Wade. Of all the undignified things, to have people talking about, you know. And . . . on top of that . . .   (*He cries hard.*)

Belinda.   What? What?

Reno.   (*He straightens up and talks as clear as possible*) If the other is bad, it may have spread. It could be worse than I want to think.

Wade.   Like . . . life-threatening worse?

Reno.   Like life-*taking* worse. Especially if it's spread.

Wade.   (*collapses in chair*) Oh, man. (*He sobs lightly.*)

Reno.   So now you know why I left the sweet little dance at Max's? Can I start a dance with someone? Talk to her, laugh with her, now? How fair is that? To anybody.

Belinda.   Reno, you don't know for sure that the worse will happen.

Reno.   No, but you think I'm going to play with someone's heart until I know?

Wade.   I'm going to take care of you.

Reno.   (*getting another drink*) Don't be ridiculous. You have a job.

Wade.   I'll take care of you at night.

Reno.   You're the Midnight Sailor.

Wade. Not anymore.

Reno. I can't let you give that up.

Wade. You had nothing to do with it. I quit last night.

Belinda. What? *Why*?

Reno. You have the most popular show in the area.

Wade. I need to be home more at night.

Reno. Yeah, right. I know you, Wade.

Wade. Not all of me.

Reno. That show is the source of your female entertainment.

Wade. No, it's not.

Reno. Oh, Wade.

Wade. It was to begin with, but it's a front now. I have to tell you something. And Belinda, you're going to hear it, too. I can't believe I am saying it, but I am. You just dropped a bombshell on us. I can't top that anyway.

Reno. (*laughing through tears*) I hope you can't.

Wade. Okay. Uh. (*thinking how to say it*) Every night when I leave the station?

Belinda. Yeah?

Wade. You know. I talk to those women on the air.

Reno. Yes?

Wade. I talk to them on the air only.

Belinda. On the air, only?

Wade. Yeah, when I leave the station . . . (*He pauses.*)

Belinda. Yes? Spit it out, Radio Stud.

Wade. I spend all my time with . . . Annie.

Reno and Belinda laugh hysterically.

Belinda.   Annie? Are you kidding?

Wade.   No. (*They realize he is not kidding.*) But don't say a *word* to her about it.
Don't tell her I said *anything*.

Reno.   But she doesn't . . . well, she acts like she doesn't. . . oh, wow.

Belinda.   You're serious?

Wade.   Very.

Belinda.   Oh, my gosh! Oh, my gosh! You and Annie . . .

Wade.   Yeah, we going to get married.

Reno.   You're getting married?

Wade.   Yes, and you, you moron, are going to be my best man.

Reno.   If I'm alive.

Wade.   Don't talk like that. You're going to be alive. Don't say that.

Belinda.   (*stretches out on the couch or the floor*) This is more information than I
can process at once.

Wade.   I'm sorry, Reno.   I know that the fact that Annie and I are in this
relationship is not as important as what you're facing, but I want you to
know that I do intend to be there for you. You need me.

Reno.   (*grabs him and cries*) I know I do. I know I do.

Wade.   Is this why you've been painting so much recently? Making a point?

Reno.   Leaving a legacy.

Belinda.   Hey, you're not dead, but, God forbid, if something did happen to you,
you already have legacy second to none.

Reno.   But my art, Belinda, my art. I've sold a few. Heck, there are a few out
now on loan. I'm hoping somebody will pick one up tomorrow morning
and ask, "Who painted this? I must know. We have to find this man!" I
know that probably won't happen, but it doesn't hurt to hope.

Belinda. Reno, don't sell yourself short.

Reno. Well, I'll sell myself anyway to be bought. For the record, there are a lot more in the back bedroom. Tons.

Wade. Of paintings?

Reno. Yeah. And drawings and a little bit of sculpture and who knows what.

Annie and Yago walk in.

Annie. Of all the ridiculous wastes of time!

Belinda. What's wrong?

Wade. What took you so long?

Annie. Mr. Police Man. I "swerved." "Crossed the line," he said.

Yago. She didn't. I was there.

Annie. Oh, yes, Yago was there. It was bad enough that we had the more arrogant lawman ever. Attitude for days. But Yago has to open his mouth. Mentioned his name. Of course. The cop thought he was drunk and talking about wine, searched the car. Took forever. Breathalyzers, walking lines. Came down to a warning for crossing the yellow line. What an tool.

Yago. We passed the tests, and that just made him madder.

Annie. And Reno, why did you leave that poor Zoe girl? When we left, she was drying tears.

Belinda. Don't worry about it, Annie.

Annie. But . . .

Reno. She'll tell you later. She has quite the story to tell herself. (*Reno, Wade, and Belinda laugh. Annie and Yago look at each other.*)

Annie. (*motioning to Yago*) Don't ever leave me with him again.

Wade. Life is short, Annie. It's way too short.

Annie. (*to Reno*) Where's your bandage?

Yago.   And your scars or blood or whatever?

Reno.   It's a long story. *(He picks up the bandage and holds it.)* A very long story. With surprising imagery. *(He laughs.)*

Yago.   What imagery?

Wade.   *(Grabbing Yago by the neck)* More than you can handle.

Belinda.   Radio Stud, Wade, how wicked! *(She laughs.)*

There is a knock at the door. Yago looks to Reno as if to ask if he should answer it. Reno nods. Before Yago gets to the door, the audience can hear Nina's voice saying, "Answer the door, Reno. It's your degenerate mother."

Reno grabs his shirt and wraps it around himself without buttoning it.

Reno.   Go ahead. Open it.

Nina comes in.

Nina.   I see you are in here with your friends, laughing, talking, all that stuff.

Reno.   Yeah, that's pretty accurate.

Nina.   Well, I won't keep you long. I just want to tell you that your step-father and step-grandmother and I are moving along. We're hitting the road. I sat in the hotel this afternoon and thought about everything, and I came to a conclusion. I'm on the road for a purpose. I don't do *this* well. Heck, I don't even like this. I haven't seen your sister in a coon's age, and I really don't know when I'll see you again, but I'm not sitting here. Whatever medical problems you had, you're right. you're grown. I didn't see your tonsils out or that whatever the operation you had when you were about twelve.

Reno.   It was knee surgery, and I was seventeen.

Nina.   Whatever. See I don't know. But I wasn't there. To be honest, I wasn't there to see my own mother leave this earth, but you were. I guess that counts. So, thank you for that. If you need me, just have the Stud email Annabelle Lee. But other than that, I'm moving on. You can handle whatever this is without me.

Belinda.   But, Mrs. Greene.

Reno.   Belinda, no.

Belinda. But . . .

Reno. No.

Nina. There you have it. I hope things go well.   I guess I'll see you when I see you.

Reno. I'll see you, Mom. (*He hugs her. She awkwardly hugs him back.*)

Nina. (*laughing*) Let go; you're holding too tight. (*He lets go.*) Bye.

Reno. Bye.

She leaves.

Belinda. Reno, are you going to . . . *(as if her question were going to be completed with the words "just let her go?")*

Reno. Yes, I am. (*The room goes silent. Reno gets five glasses together, passes them out, and pours everyone a drink.*) Here's to good news on Monday.

Belinda and Wade. Good news on Monday.

Annie and Yago. (*confused—slowly*) Good news on Monday.

They all drink.   Reno pulls the shirt around himself very tight—as if he's cold.   He exits to the bedroom.

Reno. Good news on Monday.

Lights dim.

Scene 7

Reno's porch.   It's about a month later.   He is sitting on the porch.   He looks sick and weak.   He is wearing a bandana to cover his scalp.   On the porch beside him are several paintings.   He is playing a guitar.

Yago and Wade come walking up.

Wade.   Hey, Mr. Renaissance Man!

Reno.   (*Very weak*) Hey, my favorite guys in the world!

Yago.   How you feeling, Reno.

Reno.   I'm okay, Yago. I'm not great. I'm tired, like yesterday. The chemo's really doing a number on me. Week number four. (*He laughs.*)

Wade.   Well, it's good to see you playing and singing. That's been a while.

Reno.   Yeah.

Wade.   That song new?

Reno.   Yeah. Still working on it.

Wade.   Cool.

Yago.   And more paintings. Did the nurses leave already? Need someone to get you paint?

Reno.   No, Grandma Moses is in there somewhere, at least she looks like her. She looks 140, but I'm the one dying.

Wade.   Reno . . .

Reno.   Yes, dying, Wade. It's okay. Dying.

Wade just looks at him and turns his head to keep from crying.

Yago.   Hey, but the chemo's good news!

Reno.   Want some?

Yago.   No.

Reno.   Good answer.

Wade.   (*Composing himself*) I'll be calling in the tux measurements this afternoon. Still up to being my best man?

Reno.   You have to ask?

Wade.   Good. Just making sure you're okay.

Reno.   I am very okay. Really. You know, Zoe visited for a while today.

Yago.   Really? Cool, man.

Wade.   She's a sweetheart. That's great.

Reno.   They basically have given her my job. I told her, though, that when I get back to work, I want every project back on my to-do stack. (*He laughs— and coughs.*)

Yago.   You okay?

Reno.   Yeah, Yago. I'm okay. Oh, and I got a call from Henry MacAulley about the "Lady in the Fields" painting . . .

Wade.   Yeah?

Reno.   They want to show it in the future classics' series at the college.

Wade.   That's a step, Picasso!

Yago.   Congrats, Reno.

Reno.   Thanks. I'd like . . . (*He stops and stares ahead.*)

Wade.   What? *(He looks around.)*

A young woman approaches. She is dressed nicely and is wiping her nose.

Wade.   Jaclyn?

Yago.   *(looking at her and then turning away)* Ugh. No.

Jaclyn .   Reno? Reno? Is that you? (*She starts to cry.*) Reno?

Reno.   Jaclyn. Yeah, . . . in all my glory. (*He does not smile.*)

Wade and Yago move to the side and watch.

Jaclyn.   Oh, Baby. *(She runs up on the porch and hugs him. He does not respond.)* Oh, Reno. I heard that you got sick, and I had to come see you before . . . well . . .

Reno.   Before I die?

Jaclyn. No, Baby. Well, . . . no, before you got too sick. I miss you something terrible.

Reno stares. There is a pause.

Jaclyn. Everyday. I . . . I'm not sure why I'm here. I figured . . . You deserve an explanation for all the . . . I . . . I don't how to tell you this. (*She laughs nervously.*) I got married. It was pretty soon after . . . well, after . . .

Reno. You jilted me.

Jaclyn. Well, yeah. Reno, I saved us both a lot of grief.

Reno. Saved?

Jaclyn. Let me finish, please. I got married to this guy. He was really nice and cute. . .

Reno. Did you know him before you left me?

Jaclyn. What?

Reno. I'm not a well man. It's hard to talk a lot. There's only one thing I want from you. The reason was either him or me. I asked if you knew him before you left me.

Jaclyn. Yeah, I did. But . . . oh, Reno. I don't know how to explain. I just . . . I just needed something else. I have this beautiful little girl and a handsome son, and they are the light of my life, but I still think about . . . I know that I . . . I loved Ryan so much . . . that was the man I married. And I loved him for so long . . . and I don't apologize for that . . . and yes, I knew him before I left you. I *loved* him before I left you. That's truth.

Reno. What are you wanting, Jaclyn? Why are you here? From Indiana.

Jaclyn. 'Cause you're gonna die, Reno. Die. I had to see you. And, well, so much of my life is long gone. And you're about to be gone. I wanted to see you. I . . . don't know. (*She pauses.*) Talk to me, Reno. (*She sits on the porch steps and looks up at him.*) I don't want forgiveness. Just talk to me. Once you told me that you'd tell me about the power of the human heart one day, its capacity to love and live and survive. You were going to paint me a picture about it—the strength and survival of the heart. Tell me now. Tell me about it, Reno.

Reno. Tell you? Me? I couldn't begin to tell you about the intricacies of the human heart. What makes one person feel attraction for another. What makes a man content in his own little world? What makes a mother love her children so much that every fiber of her being aches for their welfare. Or what makes another mother forget that she even has offspring for years on end. What makes people take risks with such grave possible consequences, skydiving, snake-handling, stunt work, just for the sake of holding destiny in their hands. What makes a couple fall in love with each other and live in happiness for a lifetime. What makes another couple decide after a year that it's not working. The intricacies of the human heart? Everybody else? No, I couldn't tell you. I can't look into the psyches of other people. I don't have the power to tell you why people do what they do, how they think, how they feel. To be honest, I don't even know what I feel. And how's this. I don't try to know anymore. I don't want to know. There's no need. It's the mystery of being human. And even if I did know and I was stupid enough to share, it would have to be with someone I trust and someone I want to know me, to hear me. So, you ask me about the human heart? My answer is "no."

Reno stands tall, a powerful force, and stares straight at her.

Jaclyn.   Well, Reno. I see you haven't lost your flair for words. Your answer is not "no." In fact, it's rather clear. *You* choose a path for your heart that . . .

Reno.   Good-bye, Jaclyn.

Jaclyn.   You wallow in your pain. You want to let the past dictate . . .

Reno.   Good-bye.

Jaclyn.   It doesn't matter because some of us go on to have normal lives and . . .

Wade.   Enough!

Jaclyn.   I came here to see you before you leave this world, but you'd rather . . .

Wade.   That's enough, Jaclyn. Leave.

Jaclyn looks at Reno. He remains tall. She picks up her purse.

Jaclyn.   *(to Reno)* Sweet dreams. *(to Wade)* Enjoy. *(As she walks off she speaks, forcefully and in an uncaring manner)* "Now I lay me down to sleep. I pray the Lord my soul to keep. If I should die before I wake, I ask the Lord my soul to take." *(She is gone.)*

Wade, frozen, stares at the sky above the audience. Reno remains.

Yago.   Reno, you okay?

Reno.   Yeah.

Yago.   Wade, you?

Wade.   Yeah, I'm fine.

Reno slowly steps off the porch. Yago goes and helps him.

Yago.   Talk about out of the blue!

Reno slightly grabs his abdomen.

Reno.   Yeah, and a month ago, I would have wanted it, settle it, to fix it, to . . .
                 close it. For some reason now, it's just . . . not important.

Wade.   *(Still looking up)* When I was a kid, nine, ten, I had a kite, one of those
                 really neat ones with all the angles and the colors. I loved that thing. It
                 took me forever to assemble, but man, could it fly, especially on days like
                 this. One day, though, I *really* flew it. I let out a lot more string, way too
                 much. It went up and up and got smaller and smaller, almost to the point
                 that if I didn't feel the slight tension on the cord, I would never have
                 known it was there. I knew I was in trouble when I couldn't do anything.
                 I pulled and twisted, but it was too high, too much string. I didn't know
                 whether to start yanking cord as hard as I could or to tie it to a tree and
                 leave or to just let it go. But I stayed. I tried. I pulled. Finally, I felt the
                 string give way. The kite was still attached, but it was nose-diving. I
                 wrapped string as fast as I could, trying to regain control, but it was no
                 use. I couldn't save it. It came down, and it crashed. And at that point, I
                 really didn't care. Even if it had been reparable, I still wouldn't have kept
                 it. I was tired. Very tired.

Reno bends double with pain and starts coughing.

Yago.   *(helping him)* Wade! Help me!

Wade rushes to Reno and hold him tight while he coughs.

Yago.   *(rushing inside)* I'll call the doctor.

Wade.   *(holding Reno)* Tired. *(Wade looks the sky. Reno continues to cough. The
                 lights fade.)*

Scene 8

At a gallery. A refreshment table is set up.

Yago.   (*looking behind him*) They have that sparkling grape juice, too!

Belinda.   (*sarcastically*) Good. Just what I live for. sparkling grape juice. Gimme a glass.

Yago pours two glasses.

Belinda.   (*drinking*) Not as bad as it sounds.

Yago.   This is so much fun!

Belinda.   Calm down, Yago. It's a gallery, not Mardi Gras.

Yago.   And there's Wade and Annie! Hey, you guys!

Wade and Annie approach. Wade carries a large, thin portfolio large enough to hold a painting. He leans it again the table.

Yago.   Great job! Great job! You were wonderful, Wade.

Wade.   Thank you, Yago. I guess I have to use my radio voice somewhere.

Belinda.   Happy Six Month, Anniversary, Annie. You're still beaming. I never thought I'd say that Annie is *beaming*.

Annie.   Thanks, Belinda. And I accept *beaming*. I am comfortable in it. It's not something I'd would have thought, but Wade and Annie, Mr. and Mrs. Bowman? Wade and Annie. (*thinks for a second*) Yeah, I'm *beaming*. Call me a hypocrite. (*Belinda and Annie laugh.*)

Yago.   (*to Wade*) the intricacies of the human heart, Wade? That was beautiful. I could just hear him there on that porch . . .

Wade.   Yeah. (*Hugs Yago.*)

A man approaches.

MacAulley.   Mr. Bowman. Mr. Bowman, I want to thank you for all your help in helping us get all of Mr. Brooks pieces together.

Wade.   It's Wade, Mr. MacAulley. And it was no problem. I did it for Reno. This was really his dream. He had lots of dreams, but he wanted this. Not just because he's gone or anything, but because he was talented and his paintings are good.

MacAulley. Well, Mr. Brooks' unfortunate passing in no way makes mediocre works seem better. His work is good. It was good when I met with him during his treatment, and it's still good. His death does make them more valuable monetarily, but death always inflates the good. I just wanted you to know that I appreciated your stepping in and making this run as smoothly as possible. We are fortunate to have had Mr. Brooks. And with the dealers here, more of the world will, too. *(He nods to Annie.)* Mrs. Bowman. *(He shakes Wade's hand and exits)*

Belinda. You okay, Wade?

Wade. I'm fine.

Annie. Zoe!!

Zoe approaches.

Zoe. Hi, guys! How are you?

They all greet her.

Yago. How's it going, girl?

Zoe. It's going well. Things are good. And I am so pleased that Reno's getting this exhibit. Seven of the ones in the front have already sold. Two to the same guy a New York gallery. Wade, great speech. You brought him right back to life for a while. I know I don't have nearly the memories that you do, but I do have a few, and I'll be if they're not fading! *(She smiles.)*

Wade. Well, some memories are more real than most of what we face in the present. And is that bad?

Zoe. Not at all.

Everyone repeats, "Not at all!" and raises their glasses—even if they grab one.

Wade. Belinda, may I talk with you for a minute? *(He picks up the portfolio and brings it with him to the side.)*

Belinda. Sure. What do you need, Wade? *(She follows him away from the group who continue talking.)*

Wade. For you to take this. *(He reaches in the portfolio and pulls out a painting. Belinda slowly takes it.)*

Belinda. What's this? *(She looks at it.)*

Wade. It's called . . .

Belinda. Oh, this is . . .

Wade. *Tigress.* Right there on the back.

Belinda. I was wondering where this one was. I didn't see it in the show. In fact, I haven't seen it completed. I didn't know he worked on it anymore after that night. It seems like years ago. Wow. It did turn out nice. *(She grins.)* He kept this hidden from me. I don't guess he wanted me to see it.

Wade. Well, that's not exactly true.

Belinda. I don't understand.

Wade. This is yours.

Belinda. What? No. This should go with the show—the collection.

Wade. Look at the back.

Belinda turns the painting around.

Wade. I found that last week. No name on the outside, just a small, plain, white envelope taped to the back corner. I guess he knew I'd find it . . . and pass it on.

Belinda. So, what was . . .?

Wade. Open it.

Belinda. This is odd—and so like . . . *(Wade finishes the sentence with her)* Reno! *(They both laugh. She opens up the envelope and pulls out a sheet of paper. She reads silently. As she reads, Reno, looking well, appears to the side, standing with his hands in his pockets, and recites this letter he wrote OR he sits on the floor and reads it aloud as he writes OR only his voice is heard. In any case, no one sees him. He is memory.)*

Reno. "Yes, Belinda, this is for you. Don't argue. Don't debate. I had just begun when you last saw this work. Although I had tried and tried, it took a different kind of inspiration to spark this one—and indeed them all.

77

As this painting you hold in your hand transformed and grew and matured, so did I. *(She begins to cry softy.)* The bittersweet mix of fear and thanksgiving and of uncertainty and contentment not only allowed me to face who I am; it also allowed me to believe what I could do, to be not merely a painter, but possibly an artist. So, this you hold in your hand is yours. It was inspired by you on a night I foolishly and selfishly wished to be alone, severed from a life I then thought was real. It took some aggressive compassion to wake me up. So, this painting is named after you, Tigress.

> Remember me, and live a full life,
> Reno S. Brooks
>
> P.S. You and Wade better get along for the next few
> decades, or I'll come back and haunt you both."

Belinda looks at Wade. They are both softly crying. She wipes her eyes and hugs him.

Wade.   There, there, Tigress.

Annie.   *(Sincerely)* Are you okay, Belinda?

Belinda.   Yeah, I'm good. Better than good. *(She smiles. She and Wade rejoin the group.)*

Zoe.   Oh, Belinda, did you hear me say that Annabelle Lee is moving down here? She asked me I had an extra bedroom. She said something about starting a dating service here.

Belinda.   *(regaining composure)* There you go, Yago.

Yago.   I'm content for another day or two.

Wade.   I am, too. (*He kisses Annie, walks to the side and talks in a soliloquy*) Five months, three days, and nine hours since your grand exit. I know. I know. I'm a hypocrite. We all are. I think we talked once about passions' not being complete until they consume you. Well, I feel more complete than I have in long time. (*He raises his glass.*) Here's to hope, Picasso.

Light fade and then darken.

The end.

Lowery Christopher Collins (Chris) has been an educator and writer for over thirty years. He is currently a professor of English at Panola College in Carthage, Texas. He has taught at the high school, middle school, and elementary school levels and as an English and literature instructor at the college and university level. For several years, he was a high school theatre director and a gifted education consultant. He's been honored with several teaching awards, including the Young Audiences of Northeast Texas Outstanding Service to the Profession Award and the Kennedy Center's Steven Sondheim Award for being one of the most "Inspirational Teachers" in the U.S.

He is also an award-winning playwright of over thirty scripts, a weekly newspaper columnist, a short story writer, a poet, a pianist, a vocalist, a songwriter, a recording artist with Daywind Studios, the founder and artistic director of Stagelands Theatre Company, an aspiring novelist, and a (former) choir director. He's taught a variety of classes, from rhetoric and composition to literature to acting to the Bible.

He holds a Bachelor of Arts Degree in English and History and a Master of Arts Degree in English from Stephen F. Austin State University in Texas and has served on fine arts and gifted education committees as well as on a board of governors for a small playhouse.

In addition to his interests in teaching, directing, and writing, he has a fondness for lighthouses, windmills, filmmaking, salsa, sculpture, Flannery O'Connor, travel, dominos, guacamole, social media, genetics, Maine, landscaping, pillows, gospel music, Shakespeare, marbles, YouTube, quantum physics, movies, weird jokes, maps, trees, cold rooms, and Texas.

He can be reached at mrchriscollins@hotmail.com,

on Facebook at www.facebook.com/tofferdreams,

on Twitter at "tofferdreams,"

and at his website: www.ChristopherCollinsOnline.com.

To view Christopher Collins's books and other writing, visit Ponderlake Publishing, at www.ponderlake.com.